D1643798

# 5 Minute
# TEDDY BEAR
# TALES

# Meet the Teddy Bears!

Here are some of the very fine bears you will meet in the little town of Bearborough.

# 5 Minute
# Teddy Bear
# Tales

Written by Nicola Baxter
Illustrated by Jenny Press

Published by Armadillo Books
an imprint of
Bookmart Limited
Registered Number 2372865
Desford Road
Enderby
Leicester
LE9 5AD

ISBN 1-90046-569-8

Reprinted in 1999

Produced for Bookmart Limited by Nicola Baxter
PO Box 71
Diss
Norfolk
IP22 2DT

Additional story ideas: Jenny Press
Editorial consultant: Ronne Randall
Designer: Amanda Hawkes

Printed in Singapore

# Contents

# Bedtime for Little Bears

All little bears love to snuggle down in their beds at night and go to sleep. When their little heads are on their pillows, they dream of honey and cake and teddy bear games. But before they go to bed, little bears must have their baths, and *some* little bears just do not like to get their ears wet!

Once there was a little bear called Barney, who really *hated* his bath. His father tried everything to make bathtime fun. He bought a huge boat for Barney to play with. But Barney complained that there was no room in the tub for *him*! So Barney's father bought a bottle of the biggest bubbles you have ever seen. In fact, it was fairly difficult to see that little bear at all. The bubbles floated and sparkled and burst with a *pop!* But Barney said that they tickled his nose, so they had to go.

Three yellow ducks, a water wheel, and some stuff that turned the water purple didn't work either.

One day, Barney went for a walk with his granny. As they walked, it started to rain. Luckily, Barney was wearing his boots and Granny was carrying her umbrella. But right away, Barney started to complain.

"I don't like getting wet," he whined. "It gets in my ears and in my eyes and up my nose, and it's *horrible*."

"Well, Barney, I am surprised," said Granny, "that you would want to give up all that good luck."

"Good luck?" asked Barney. "What do you mean?"

"I thought all little bears knew about it," Granny replied. "Didn't you know that every drop of water that touches you is a little bit of good luck that will follow you all your life? I always try to get as wet as possible." And Granny threw away her umbrella and started to splash in the puddles!

The next night at bathtime, Barney's father was surprised to find that Barney jumped right into the tub with no fuss at all. In fact, it was difficult to make him get out and snuggle down in his little bed. And I have heard that nowadays Barney is the luckiest little bear you have ever met—and the cleanest!

# Big Bears, Little Bears

One afternoon, Barney and his friend Cleo were playing in the park, when some bigger bears came along.

"We want to play on the swings, baby bears," they said rudely. "Get lost!"

Barney was not a very brave little bear, but he didn't want to look silly in front of Cleo, so he spoke up loudly.

"We were here first," he said, "but we could go on the merry-go-round instead, if you like. We've been on the swings for a long time now."

But as soon as Barney and Cleo were whizzing around on the merry-go-round, the bigger bears came along and wanted to play on that too. They weren't nice about it.

Cleo didn't want any trouble. "Let's go and play with our kite, Barney," she said. "They can have the swings and the merry-go-round and everything to themselves."

Barney agreed at once.

Soon the little bears were playing happily. It was a windy day that was perfect for kite-flying. But before long, the big bears began to run around playing ball. The park was plenty big enough for everyone, but they insisted on running close to the little bears. Barney was afraid that one of them would get tangled up in the kite string, or worse still, bump into him so that he let go and his kite went flying off by itself.

Just then, there was a huge gust of wind, and things happened at once. The big bears' ball blew under the merry-go-round and the little bears' kite flew into a tree. Now neither the little bears nor the big bears could play.

Barney was ready to start for home, but Cleo, who was a very clever little bear, had an idea.

"You big bears are tall enough to reach our kite," she said. "And we are small enough to crawl under the merry-go-round and get your ball. What do you think?"

The big bears shuffled their feet and looked ashamed.

"We're sorry we teased you," they said. "It's a very good idea."

So the little bears crawled, and the big bears stretched, and everyone played happily together for the rest of the afternoon.

# The Blue Bear

In a neat little house in the middle of Bearborough there lived a very silly bear. The problem with Albert was that he always had to have the very latest things. He was so eager to keep up with fashion that when he saw his friends and relatives he would say, "Oh dear, my cousin Jackson is wearing last month's jacket. Only three buttons instead of six on his coat, too. Poor Jackson. Poor bear!"

To be fair, Albert's clothes were sometimes extraordinarily wonderful, but more often he simply looked extraordinarily silly.

Each month, Albert's fashion magazines arrived in the mail. Usually they confirmed that he was the best dressed bear in town. On this particular morning, Albert couldn't wait to tear open the enormous package of magazines that had just arrived.

But when he glanced at the covers, he gave a groan of despair. *Blue!* Everything must be blue! It seemed that nothing else would do at all.

Albert looked at his wardrobe with tears in his eyes. There were orange clothes and purple clothes. There were green and yellow striped hats and pink and black spotted socks. All of them would have to go! What a waste!

But that evening in bed, Albert had an inspiration. What if he could dye all his clothes? Then he would be the height of fashion without spending too much money. It was brilliant!

Albert had so many clothes, he decided that only the ornamental pool in his garden would be big enough to dye them in. Luckily, there were no fish in it. Albert tipped in pack after pack of dye. The water became bright blue. Then he hurried to his bedroom to begin carrying out the clothes.

It was unfortunate that he tried to carry so many at once. It was even more unfortunate that he had left a watering can on the path. Before he could stop himself, Albert was sailing through the air to land with a *splash!* in the pond.

You can guess what happened. Albert was dyed blue from ears to paws. At last, thought his friends, trying not to laugh, he will have learned his lesson about keeping up with fashion.

But Albert's friends were wrong. Albert loved his new blue fur —for a while. I hear now that fashion has changed, and stripes are all the rage. Let me put it this way . . . you won't find it hard to spot Albert next time you come to Bearborough!

# The Bear on the Bus

Wednesday was market day in Bearborough. From all the surrounding farms and villages, bears flooded into town. Of course, bears came to town in all sorts of ways. They wobbled on bicycles and tricycles. They rattled along in vans and trucks. But lots of bears hopped onto the bus, which was always full to bursting.

One Wednesday morning, Barney and his granny caught the bus into town. They had a lovely time. When it was time to come home, they once again waited for the bus and squeezed onto it with lots of other bears.

"It's standing room only, I'm afraid," said Granny, "but I'll hold you up if you like, Barney, so you can see out of the window."

But Barney soon found that the bear standing in front of him was much more interesting than what was outside the windows. He was an elderly bear, wearing a hat. That was

not very strange, for lots of older bears wear hats. What *was* very odd was that Barney was sure he had seen the hat move!

Barney looked hard at the back of the bear's head. There it was again! The hat gave a little jiggle, as though it was dancing.

Barney was fascinated. The hat jiggled again. The little bear wriggled in Granny's arms with excitement.

"Keep still, Barney," said Granny. "I'll drop you if you're not careful."

"But Granny," whispered Barney, "look!" And he pointed at the bear's hat.

Just then, the hat seemed to bounce on the bear's head. Granny was so surprised that she gave a little scream, and the bear in front turned around.

"My dear lady," he cried, "can I help you in any way?"

Wordlessly, Granny pointed to his hat. The bear smiled. "I should introduce myself," he said. "I am Bertram Bear, and this," he went on, gallantly doffing his hat, "is my friend Percival."

Granny and Barney laughed aloud when they saw the little mouse sitting on the old bear's head.

"I hope that we will all be the best of friends," said Bertram, smiling at Granny.

# Teddy Bear Time

When a visitor to Bearborough last year forgot to put on her watch, she asked some local bears the time—and she got some strange answers.

"Half past three," the bear who sells fruit and vegetables said, glancing up at the Town Hall clock.

"A quarter to nine," the bear in the bakery replied, looking at the clock high on the church.

"Nine minutes after five," the bear who sells ice cream on the corner of the main street said, peering at the clock in front of the train station.

You have probably guessed that all the clocks in Bearborough were wrong. That was because old Mr. Minim, the only clock mender in town, had become a little shaky on his legs. Although fit and well in every other way, he simply could not face climbing up a ladder to mend clocks high up.

As you can imagine, the clocks really were a problem. The trains were never on time, and the shopkeepers didn't know when to open their shops.

Then, one day, Bearborough had two very special visitors. They were a bear called Alfred and his friend Jumble—who was an elephant! Now most bears in Bearborough had never seen an elephant before, so they all gathered round. And the elephant, pleased to show off his size and strength, wrapped his trunk around each of the little bears in turn and lifted them up high, squealing with excitement.

"Excuse me, Jumble," said Mr. Minim, tapping him lightly on the toe with his walking stick. "Could you lift a grown-up bear, like me, for example?"

In seconds, Mr. Minim found himself dangling above the crowd, yet he felt as safe as if he was standing on firm ground.

And that is why, if you visit Bearborough these days, all the clocks are exactly right, for Jumble visits every twelve months, and Mr. Minim always says that's the *high*light of his year!

# Uncle Hugo's Invention

Cleo's Uncle Hugo lived in a ramshackle old house on the edge of Bearborough. When Cleo first took him to visit, Barney was rather afraid of the old bear. He wasn't used to bears who talked in gruff voices and didn't seem to know what day of the week it was.

But Barney soon found that Uncle Hugo's house was one of the most exciting he had ever been in. There was a stuffed alligator in the hall and a real live parrot in the living room. There were collections of fossils and piles of books everywhere. For Uncle Hugo was the kind of bear who gets very enthusiastic about something—before he forgets all about it.

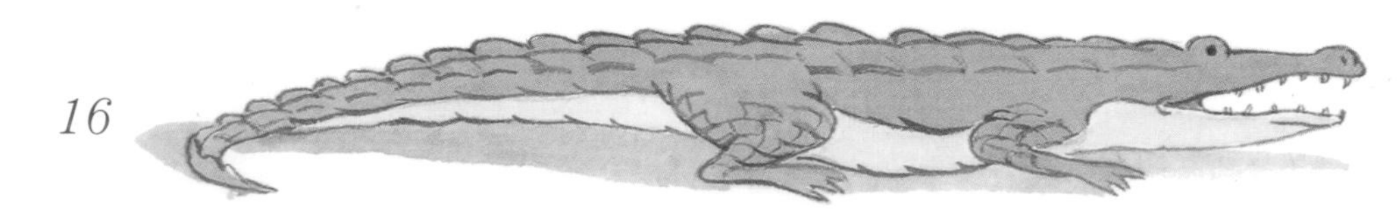

At the moment, Uncle Hugo was passionate about his new invention. It was the most extraordinary-looking machine.

"Er . . . excuse me, sir," stammered Barney. "What exactly does it do?"

"It whistles," said Uncle Hugo briefly.

"Whistles?" Cleo was just as puzzled.

"Yes," said her uncle. "I got the idea when the kettle boiled one day. It made a lovely whistling noise, so I thought I could make a machine that would whistle in tune."

Neither Barney nor Cleo was very good at whistling. The machine sounded wonderful.

"Now," cried Uncle Hugo, "for the moment of truth. I turn this switch here, and open this valve here, and the water in the boiler will start to bubble and steam. Then prepare yourselves for a wonderful sound."

Sure enough, there soon came a bubbling, followed by a whooshing, and then, yes, there was a sound that would make any young bear grin with delight. But it wasn't the sound of whistling. Oh no. It was the sound of Uncle Hugo zooming across the room on his machine and crashing straight through the doors that led into the garden.

When Barney and Cleo rushed outside, they found Uncle Hugo and his machine sitting in the middle of a rose bed.

"Hmm," said the old bear. "It's not, in fact, a whistling machine after all. It's a steam-driven mowing machine, and it works perfectly! Just look at my lawn!"

And Uncle Hugo was so happy that he began to . . . whistle.

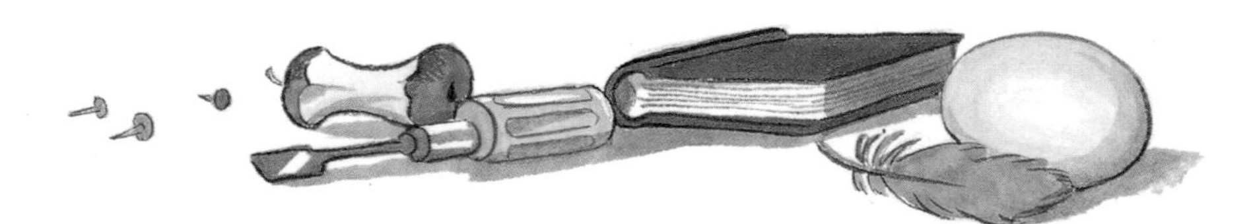

# The Snow Bear

When heavy snow fell on the town of Bearborough, Cleo's little brother really wanted to go out and play in it. But he still had a bad cold, so Cleo's mother said he must stay indoors.

"Don't worry, Max," said Cleo kindly. "I'll build you a beautiful snow bear right in front of the window where you can see it all day."

No sooner had Cleo started piling up the snow, when Barney came past, pulling his sled.

"Can I play too?" he asked. "I bet I could build a better snow bear than you!"

"Just you come and try!" retorted Cleo.

Well, before long, several other little bears came along.

"What are you doing?" they called.

"We're having a snow bear competition," cried Barney. "Come and join us!"

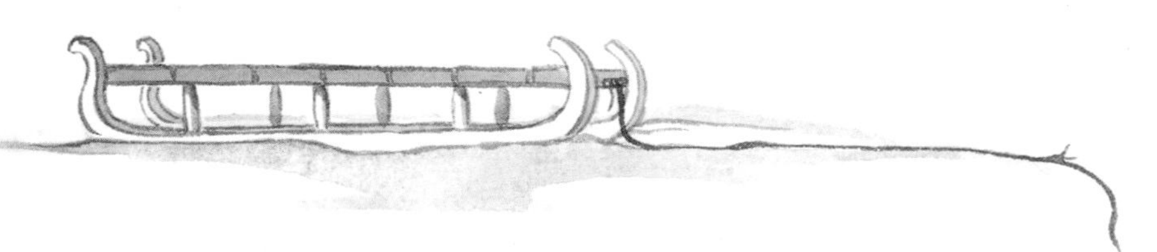

Soon, much to Max's delight, there were five little bears building snow bears in Cleo's garden.

Everyone was very busy—except Barney. He soon decided to take a rest by throwing snowballs into the branches of the trees. It was fun when the snow lying high up came down with a *whoosh!* The other little bears were too busy making their snow bears to notice.

After about an hour, the bears had finished. Five fine snow bears stood in a row in the garden. Cleo's mother agreed to be the judge of the competition, and Max pointed excitedly to help her make the right choice.

"There's no doubt about it," she said after a careful look at the snow bears. "The one at the end is certainly the best."

"It must be Barney's bear," said Cleo, "but where is he?"

Just then, there was a muffled giggle, and Barney's bear collapsed in a heap—with Barney inside it!

"The snow from that tree fell right on top of me," he laughed. "Didn't I make a good snow bear?"

"I can't award a prize for an accident!" laughed Cleo's mother. "You can all have a prize of hot cocoa. Come inside now!"

# Follow the Rainbow

On Saturday mornings, lots of little bears went to the library for Story Time. Mr. Leaf, the librarian, asked them all to sit down in a circle, while he read to them from one of the beautiful books on the shelves.

One morning, Mr. Leaf read a story in which a pixie found a pot of gold at the end of a rainbow. Barney was very interested, especially when he noticed that it was raining outside.

When the children were ready to go home, the rain had stopped, although there were lots of lovely puddles for them to splash in.

But Barney didn't want to stop and splash. "Come on!" he said to Cleo, pulling her along. "We've got to hurry!" And he dragged the poor little bear along Main Street.

As soon as the tallest buildings were left behind, the two bears could see that there was a beautiful rainbow in the sky.

"Quick!" cried Barney. "We've got to find the end before it disappears!"

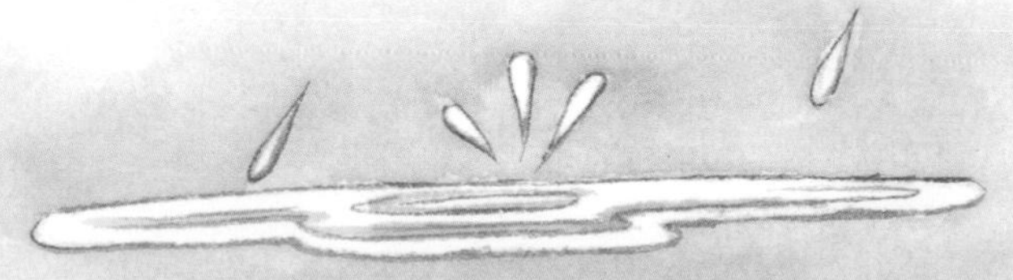

"But Barney! . . ." Cleo's sensible words were lost as her friend rushed along.

"Look!" cried Barney a few moments later. He could hardly believe his eyes. There was no doubt about it. As they reached the top of the hill that led down to Barney's house, they could clearly see the end of the rainbow. And it was right in the middle of his front garden!

Barney and Cleo flew down the hill, but as they reached the front gate, something very odd happened. The rainbow disappeared!

"We're too late!" sighed Cleo.

But Barney was not ready to give up yet. "The rainbow is gone," he said, "but maybe the pot of gold is still there. Where's my shovel?"

And before Cleo could stop him, the silly little bear was busy digging up his father's beloved tulip bed.

Just at that moment, Barney's father came out of the house. "Stop right there, young bear!" he called. He didn't sound happy.

But as he spoke, something shiny went *clink!* on Barney's shovel and came flying toward his father.

Mr. Bear caught it in one large paw.

"Why, goodness me," he said, "it's the ring I lost when I was weeding last year!"

After that, Mr. Bear didn't have the heart to be cross with Barney.

"Maybe rainbows do have gold at the end of them," he laughed. "Let me know when you see another one, Barney!"

# Mother Bear's Problem

One morning, Mother Bear had a worried look on her furry face. "I know there's something I'm supposed to remember about today," she said, "but I can't for the life of me think what it is. I'm pretty sure it's something important."

"It's my birthday!" suggested Barney hopefully.

"Don't be silly," said his mother. "That's in October."

"It's *your* birthday!" Barney was trying to help.

"I think," said Mother Bear coldly, "I'd remember my own birthday, Barney. I may have forgotten one little thing, but I haven't completely lost my senses."

But Mother Bear was still worried. She checked her calendar to make sure that it wasn't time for her dentist's appointment, or Barney's school concert, or Mr. Bear's fishing contest. She went through her papers to make sure that her bills were paid. She looked in the washing machine to see if there was laundry to be hung out or ironed. Still she knew that she had not remembered the thing she had forgotten.

"Never mind," said Mr. Bear at lunchtime. "If we have nothing else to do this afternoon, let's watch that old film on television. We can put our feet up and relax."

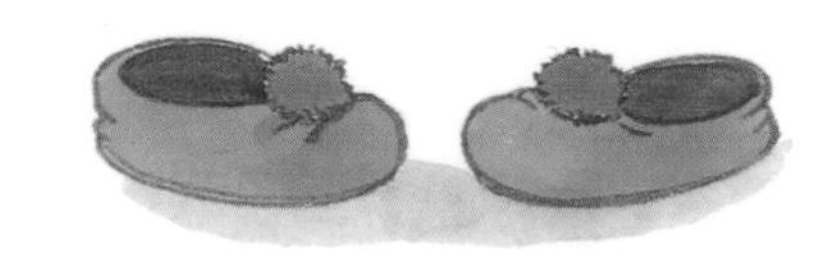

By half-past three, Mother Bear and her husband were settled on the sofa with mugs of coffee, a box of chocolates, and wearing their oldest, comfiest slippers (which in Mr. Bear's case were almost antiques!).

The film was so exciting that Mother Bear almost forgot about her problem, until . . . *Driiiiiiiiing!* . . . there came a ring at the doorbell.

Mother Bear felt a sinking feeling in her tummy that had nothing to do with eating too many chocolates.

"Hello, darlings!" called Aunt Hortense, opening the door herself with a flourish. "I've come to stay until Monday as I promised," she said, from under her huge hat.

"I've remembered what I forgot," groaned Mother Bear to Mr. Bear, too softly for Aunt Hortense to hear. "I was going to suggest that we all went away for the weekend!"

# How Many Paws?

One fine day, several little bears and their parents set off for a picnic at the beach. The grown-up bears carried huge baskets of goodies, while the little bears had almost as much to carry, since they had brought every pail and shovel they could find.

"Phew!" said Barney's father, when they reached the beach at last. "You little bears can start making sandcastles, while we get everything ready for lunch."

But it was such a wonderful, sunny day that almost all the grown-up bears had fallen fast asleep before the little bears had really started on their sandcastles.

"Look!" said Bettina, a very naughty little bear, "while they are sleeping, we could have just a little taste of the picnic."

Although most of the little bears were usually good little bears, that did sound like a very good idea. Barney peeked into the nearest basket, which had a missing strap, and saw a plastic box. With just a little twist of his paw, he managed to lift off the lid. Inside was a big chocolate cake!

One by one, the little bears squeezed their paws into the basket and took a taste of the cake. It was the yummiest cake they had ever tasted, and it somehow was even more delicious because they could only eat a tiny bit of it at one time.

It wasn't very long before all that was left of the cake was a pile of sticky crumbs.

"Quick!" said Bettina. "We'd better start making our sandcastles right now, or the grown-ups will wonder what we've been doing."

So when the grown-up bears awoke from their snooze a few minutes later, they found themselves surrounded by fine sandcastles. And not long after that, they found themselves missing one very fine chocolate cake.

"Oh dear," said Barney, shaking his head sadly. "I suppose it will be almost impossible to find out whether it was taken by seagulls or crabs or . . . er . . . turtles."

"Or bears!" said his father. "I'm happy to say that it will be very easy to find out who has eaten the cake, because the chocolate has made lots of sand stick to their paws and noses!"

# The Star Bears

Late at night, when all his clocks were striking twelve, Mr. Minim the clock mender loved to sit at his bedroom window and look at the stars. Nowadays, he found that he did not need as much sleep as he once did. Looking out at the little sparkling lights in the sky passed the time wonderfully.

Ever since he was a very young bear, Mr. Minim had loved the night sky. His wise old grandfather had told him the names of all the groups of stars, and Mr. Minim could still remember every one of them.

"I wish the young bears today were interested in astronomy," said Mr. Minim to himself.

Next morning, Mrs. Bear and Barney came into Mr. Minim's shop. Mrs. Bear had brought her best clock to be mended.

"It used to keep time beautifully," she said, "but last night it was almost midnight before Barney went upstairs to bed because the clock was wrong."

"Almost midnight?" said Mr. Minim. "Then you must have seen the star bears."

"I did see the stars," said Barney, "but I didn't see any bears."

"That's because you didn't know where to look," said Mr. Minim. "You need someone to show you—perhaps your daddy or Mrs. Bear here."

"I'm afraid my husband and I wouldn't know where to look either," said Mrs. Bear. "Perhaps you could come and show us one fine night."

"I'll bring your clock back tonight," said Mr. Minim. "Will ten o'clock be all right?"

"Oh yes!" cried Barney, who loved to stay up late.

That night, Mr. Minim showed the whole Bear family lots of interesting things about the night sky. Best of all, he showed them the star bears.

"There's the Great Bear," he said, "and there's the Little Bear."

"Is he older than me?" asked Barney.

"Young bear," laughed Mr. Minim, "he's even older than *me*! And that really *is* old!"

# The Lost Ribbon

In many ways, thought Cleo, Emmeline Bruin was the most annoying bear at school. All that Emmeline cared about was looking pretty. She wouldn't join in any rough games in case the frills on her dress got torn. She wouldn't play in the sand in case her paws got dirty. In fact, she was no fun at all.

"I'm never going to be good friends with Emmeline," Cleo told Barney one day on the way home from school. "She doesn't care about anyone but herself."

The very next day at school, all the little bears went on a nature walk with their teacher, Mr. Tedson. They were supposed to be looking carefully at trees and picking up any leaves that had fallen to the ground.

"The shape of the leaf will tell you what kind of tree it has come from," said Mr. Tedson.

But the little bears had not been in the woods for long before Emmeline began to wail.

"I've lost my ribbon!" she sobbed. "It was my best red ribbon!"

Cleo had always thought that Emmeline looked a little silly with a big bow between her ears, but with the other bears, she began hunting for the lost ribbon.

In fact, it was Cleo who found it first. At least, she was the first to see where it was. In a little bush beside the path, a tiny bird was busy weaving the ribbon into her nest. Cleo could see at once that pulling out the ribbon would destroy the nest.

Cleo was about to turn away, determined never to tell anyone what she had seen, when she heard a sound behind her. It was Emmeline! Cleo held her breath. That spoiled little bear was sure to make a fuss and demand her ribbon back.

But Emmeline was smiling. "Let's not say anything," she whispered. "It looks much prettier there than on my head!" And she smiled at Cleo.

Cleo smiled back. You can't always tell what someone is like just by looking at them, she thought. And she knew right there and then that she and Emmeline were going to be the very best of friends after all.

# Cousin Carlotta

One morning, Mrs. Bear got a letter. "It's an invitation," she said, "to a Grand Ball given by Mrs. Carlotta Carmody. I've never heard of her!"

"You must know her," cried Mr. Bear. "I've never been to a Grand Ball, and I'd like to go to this one."

"We can't go to a party given by someone we don't know," said Mrs. Bear. "And the name doesn't sound familiar at all."

"Look, there's some writing on the back!" cried Barney, who had been peering up at the invitation.

Mrs. Bear turned the invitation over. Scribbled on the back was a short message. "Dear Cousin, Yes, this is me, little Carly! I've married James Justin Jackson Carmody III. Do come to our party!"

"I don't believe it!" cried Mrs. Bear. "Cousin Carly was the scruffiest, untidiest, and, quite honestly, the messiest bear I ever knew. The very idea of that harum-scarum bear in a ball gown is quite beyond me. But we shall have to go, of course."

"Oh, of course," smiled her husband.

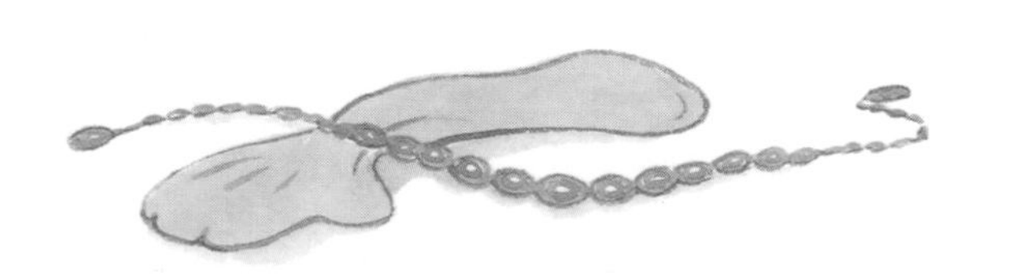

Three weeks later, the Bear family, dressed in their finest clothes, arrived at Cousin Carlotta Carmody's mansion. It was huge!

"I feel faint," said Mrs. Bear. "Barney, there will be no running about, no jumping, and definitely no sliding down stairs. Do you understand?"

"Yes," said Barney, looking regretfully at the wonderfully long and curving banisters.

All the guests were gathered in the hall, waiting for their hostess to make her grand entrance.

Suddenly, there was a chandelier-jingling yell.

"*Wheeeeeeeeeee!*" Cousin Carlotta made a grand entrance, all right—sliding down the banisters! Unfortunately, she left most of her train dangling from a picture frame, and her tiara was over one eye by the time she reached the bottom.

Mrs. Bear forgot her nerves in a second. She ran forward to help her cousin to her feet.

"Carly," she smiled, "you haven't changed a bit!"

# The Bear on the Stairs

The Bear family enjoyed Cousin Carlotta's party enormously, but they did not have much chance to look around her beautiful house—there was simply too much dancing and eating and talking to be done!

"Darlings, you must come back next week for a proper visit," said Carlotta, as the Bears left, well after midnight.

"We would be delighted," said Mrs. Bear quickly. She adored looking around other people's homes.

Only Barney was not so sure that he wanted to go. He wasn't very interested in carpets and curtains.

The following Saturday, the Bear family arrived just before lunch. They had a splendid meal in the very fine dining room, then Mr. and Mrs. Bear set off with Carlotta for the Grand Tour.

"I think I'll stay here," said Barney, "and . . . er . . . look at the pictures."

Barney wandered around for a while, before going to sit on the grand staircase. He felt very bored and let out a big sigh.

"You could play with me, if you like," said a little bear on the stair above.

Barney jumped. He hadn't even noticed the bear, who was wearing strange clothes, made out of some shiny stuff. But he looked like a friendly little bear, and pretty soon Barney and the bear, who said that his name was Charles, were playing a wonderful game running up and down the hallway. Barney couldn't remember when he had had so much fun.

"There you are!" came his father's voice suddenly. "I hope you've been behaving yourself, Barney."

"Oh yes," said his son. "I've been playing with Ch..." and he turned to introduce his friend. But the little bear was nowhere to be seen.

Cousin Carlotta looked at Barney strangely. "What did the little bear look like?" she asked.

Barney hesitated, looking around for inspiration. Then, suddenly, he saw a large picture of Charles on the wall.

"That's him," he said. "That's my friend Charles."

Carlotta smiled. "That's my husband's great-great-great-grandfather," she said. "He lived over two hundred years ago—but he does like to make sure that young visitors feel at home!"

# A Bear's Best Friend

One year, an uncle who lived overseas very unwisely gave Cleo a joke book for her birthday. It was dreadful. All day long, Cleo was trying out the jokes on her friends and family. And most of them were not very funny at all.

"What do you call a sleeping dinosaur?" she asked her father.

"I don't know, Cleo," groaned her long-suffering dad. "What do you call a sleeping dinosaur?"

"A brontosnorus!" chortled Cleo. "What goes clomp, clomp, clomp, clomp, clomp, clomp, clomp, squoosh?"

"I'll make you go squoosh, if you're not careful," grunted her father. "I don't know. What does go clomp, clomp, clomp, clomp, clomp, clomp, clomp, squoosh?"

"An octopus with one shoe off!" Cleo couldn't stop giggling. "What does Tarzan sing at Christmastime?"

"You're not still asking those awful jokes, are you, Cleo?" asked her mother, coming in at that moment. "I don't know. What does Tarzan sing at Christmastime?"

"Jungle bells! Jungle bells!" sang Cleo, waving her book in the air.

"Cleo! We didn't think they could get worse, but they have!" cried her parents together. "How many more pages are there?"

"Oh, hundreds!" laughed Cleo, looking at her book. "Who is a bear's best friend?"

Cleo's mother sank into a chair. "I don't know," she sighed wearily. "Who is a bear's best friend?"

Cleo turned the page, and gave a little cry. "Oh, they've forgotten to put in the answer!"

"That's fine, Cleo," replied her father, leaping out of his chair, "because for once I know the punch line to that joke. Who is a bear's best friend? It's the very sensible grown-up bear who takes away her joke book while some of her friends and family are still speaking to her!" And in two big strides, he'd grabbed the book and carried it away to his shed in the backyard.

Unfortunately, that was this morning, and Cleo's father has not been seen since, although the most extraordinary sounds have been coming from the shed. If I didn't know better, I'd say they were giggles!

# The Striped Scarf

One frosty afternoon, Mr. Bear came in for lunch rubbing his paws. "It's so cold out there," he said, "I thought my ears would fall off."

Barney looked anxiously at his father's ears, but they looked fine.

"What I need," said Mr. Bear carelessly, knowing that his birthday was just a few weeks away, "is a nice long scarf to wrap around my neck *and* my ears."

Just as carelessly, Mrs. Bear asked her husband, "Is there any particular way that you would like the scarf to look?"

"Well, it should definitely be red," said Mr. Bear. "I've always looked good in red."

Over the next few days, Barney noticed that his mother's workbag was more bulging than usual, and just occasionally he caught sight of a tiny strand of red wool.

Mrs. Bear was right on schedule until the day that Miss Bouquet in the flower shop complimented Mr. Bear on the blue sweater he was wearing.

"You know," said Mr. Bear later, "I think if I *were* to have a scarf, it should probably be blue."

Mrs. Bear groaned. It was too late to start again. But Barney had a bright idea.

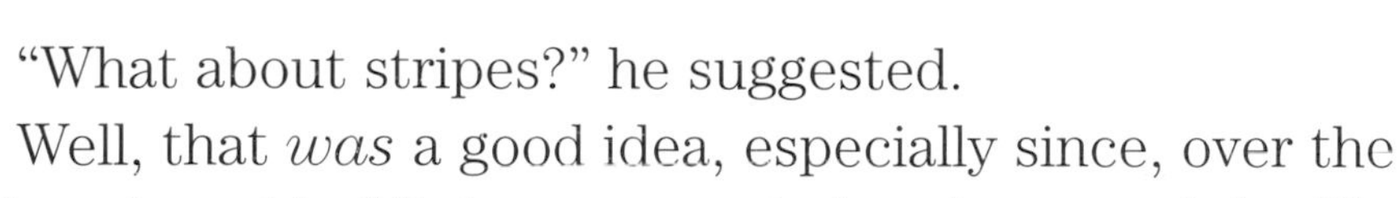

"What about stripes?" he suggested.

Well, that *was* a good idea, especially since, over the next few days, Mr. Minim commented on how much he liked Mr. Bear's yellow shirt, Mr. Leaf asked where he could get a green tie just like Mr. Bear's, and Barney, without thinking, asked if he could borrow his father's orange woolly hat. Mrs. Bear made several trips to the wool shop, and her workbag was soon more bulging than ever.

On his birthday morning, Mr. Bear felt a little anxious. What if his hints had gone unnoticed? He needn't have worried. Not only did he open the brightest scarf you have ever seen, but it was the longest, too!

"I think we're going to have to share this," laughed Mr. Bear. "Look, it's long enough to wrap around the whole family!"

# Paws with Patches

One day in a storybook, Cleo saw a picture of a bear with patches on his paws. She ran to her mother at once.

"Oh, please tell me, what has happened to this poor bear's paws? They've got bits and pieces sewn on all over them."

Her mother was busy working out her finances, but she glanced at the book and smiled.

"Oh, that's nothing to worry about. It's just a bear who has done a lot of work with his paws, so they have worn out. A kind friend has sewn some patches on for him. Now hurry along and set the table for me. I must add these figures up before we eat."

But Cleo didn't help her mother. She folded her arms and sat down in a chair.

A few minutes later, her mother looked up. "Will you do as I asked, Cleo, please?"

"No!" said Cleo.

The older bear could hardly believe her ears. Even Cleo's little brother looked up from where he was playing on the floor. Cleo was usually such a good little bear.

"Well, will you go and get your father?" Cleo's mother tried again.

"No," said Cleo.

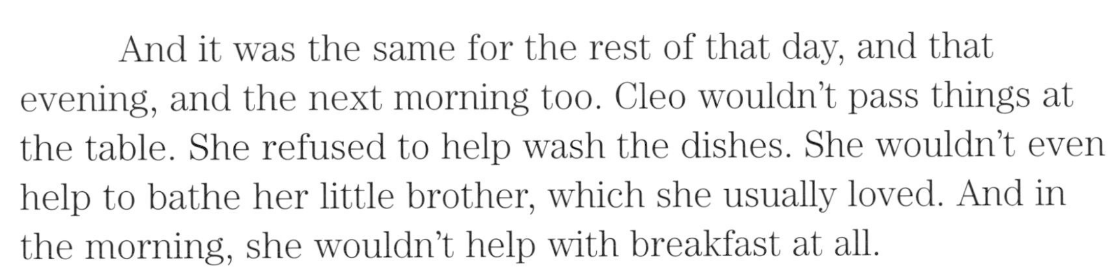

And it was the same for the rest of that day, and that evening, and the next morning too. Cleo wouldn't pass things at the table. She refused to help wash the dishes. She wouldn't even help to bathe her little brother, which she usually loved. And in the morning, she wouldn't help with breakfast at all.

Cleo went to nursery school and came back with a note from the teacher to say that she had been difficult and quite unlike her usual self.

"Sit down, Cleo," said her mother. "We need to have a serious talk."

It wasn't very long before Cleo explained everything. "I just don't want my paws to wear out," she said, "so I'm saving them."

Cleo's mother laughed. "I'm surprised about that," she said, "considering how much most bears *want* patches on their paws."

"Do they?"

"Oh yes, it's like wearing a medal. It shows what a long and useful life you've led," explained her mother.

Well, ever since then, Cleo has been a *very* helpful little bear, though her paws look perfect to me!

# The Singing Bear

If you walk along the main street of Bearborough at six o'clock in the morning, there is usually very little going on. On Wednesdays, of course, when there is a market, there may already be a few stallholders setting out their goods, but most of the week, Bearborough is a very quiet place.

And that is why it was so shocking when the singing began. Yes, singing. At about six o'clock, when most bears are still tucked up in their beds, a sound would ring out across the square.

*TRA-la-la-la-la-la-la-LAAAAA!*

It wasn't a horrible sound. In fact, it was quite a lovely sound. But it wasn't the kind of thing you expect to hear when your ears are still snuggled in your pillow.

The first morning that this happened, bears shook their heads and thought they were dreaming. But by the third morning, bears dressed in a strange assortment of nightclothes gathered in the street to try to stop the disturbance.

*TRA-la-la-la-la-la-la-LAAAAA!*

"It can't go on!" cried Mr. Minim. "I need my sleep!"

"Tell me about it!" Mrs. Cuddles had baby twins who were often hard to settle.

"But listen!" fashionable Albert held up his paw. "It's beautiful, isn't it?"

And sure enough, when everyone listened hard, they realized that it was the most glorious sound they had ever heard coming from the mouth of a bear.

*TRA-la-la-la-la-la-la-LAAAAA! La-LA! La-LA!*

Mr. Leaf the librarian put his head out of his front door and cleared his throat.

"It's my sister," he said. "She's an opera singer. Her stage name is Ursula Pallas. You may have heard of her. She's staying with me for a week, and I'm afraid she has to rehearse."

Ursula Pallas? In Bearborough? *The* Ursula Pallas? The bears were stunned.

"O-o-of course she must be allowed to sing," stammered Mr. Minim. "She's the greatest singer in the world."

Even Mrs. Cuddles admitted this was true.

At that moment, one of Mr. Leaf's windows was thrown open and a famous face appeared.

"Darlings!" cried La Pallas. "I will perform especially for you, here in the square, tonight at seven."

The concert is still talked of in Bearborough. And they say that if you are very quiet, you can still hear the great Pallas's extraordinary voice echoing softly around the square.

# Bear Facts

Barney and Cleo were having supper at Barney's house. Cleo's mother had told her that she must try to think of interesting things to talk about, so that everyone would think she was a polite guest and would invite her again.

"Did you know, Mr. Bear," Cleo began, "that bears are related to raccoons?"

"Raccoons?" replied Barney's father in surprise. "Oh, I don't think so, Cleo. They're very different from us."

"No, it's true," said Cleo politely. "I read about it in my Encyclopedia of Bears."

"Really?" Mr. Bear usually liked to know best about everything, so he tried to think of something that Cleo might not know.

"Did you know that there are white bears who live on the ice all the time?" he asked.

"Oh, yes," said Cleo. "They're called polar bears and they live on fish. I had one as a penpal once, but his writing was a bit hard to read."

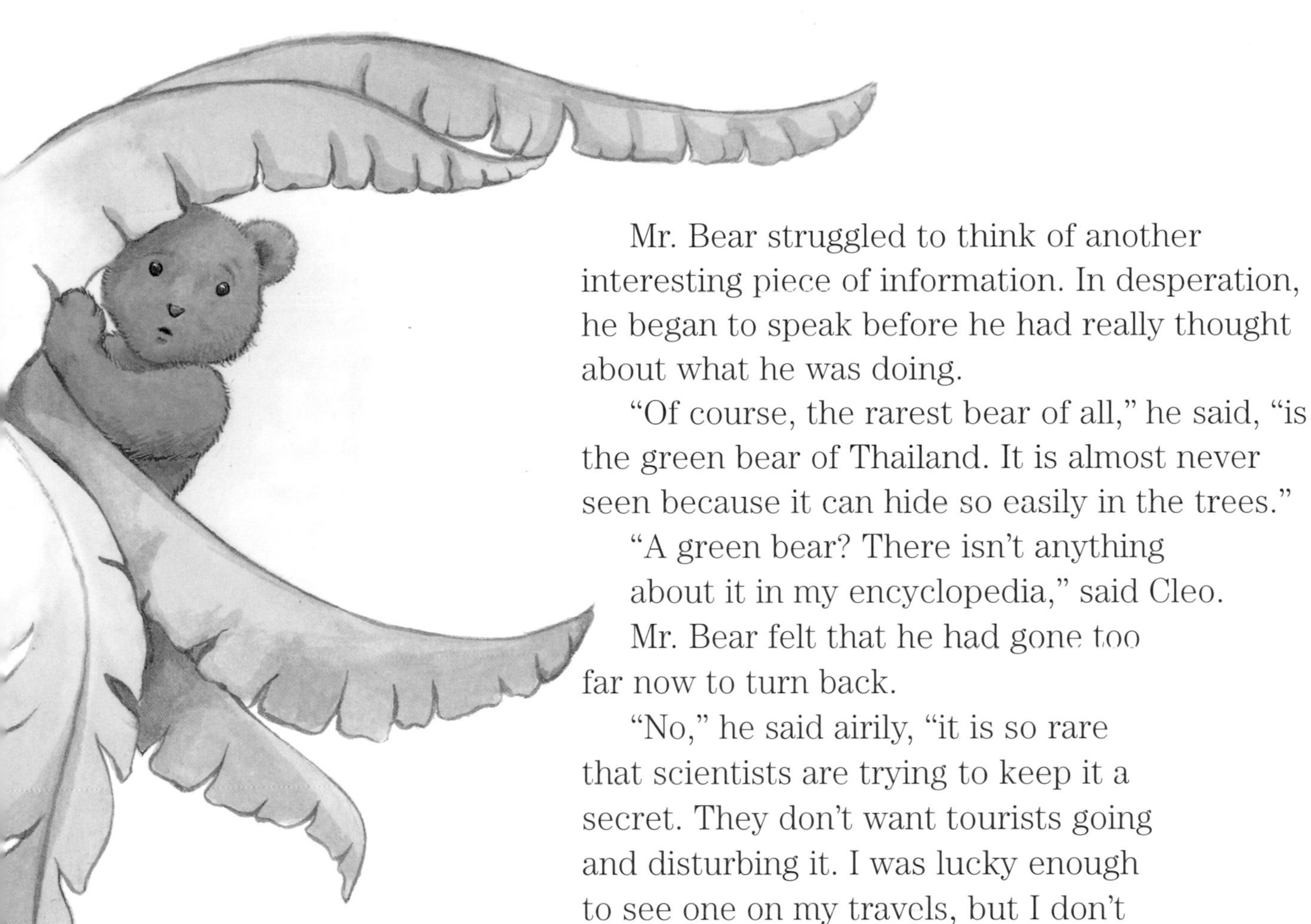

Mr. Bear struggled to think of another interesting piece of information. In desperation, he began to speak before he had really thought about what he was doing.

"Of course, the rarest bear of all," he said, "is the green bear of Thailand. It is almost never seen because it can hide so easily in the trees."

"A green bear? There isn't anything about it in my encyclopedia," said Cleo.

Mr. Bear felt that he had gone too far now to turn back.

"No," he said airily, "it is so rare that scientists are trying to keep it a secret. They don't want tourists going and disturbing it. I was lucky enough to see one on my travels, but I don't usually talk about it."

Mrs. Bear coughed loudly at the other end of the table.

"Your travels, darling?" she said sweetly. "When was that?"

"Oh, long before I met you, honey," said Mr. Bear, "when I was a young bear, you know."

"Cleo," said Mrs. Bear, "I feel I should warn you that there are bear facts and then there are what are known as bear-faced lies. You can't believe everything you hear."

"Oh, don't worry Mrs. Bear," said Cleo with dreadful honesty. "I don't believe everything that old bears say. After all, their brains go all mushy, don't they?"

"That's very true," laughed Mrs. Bear, as her husband hurried off to hide his confusion.

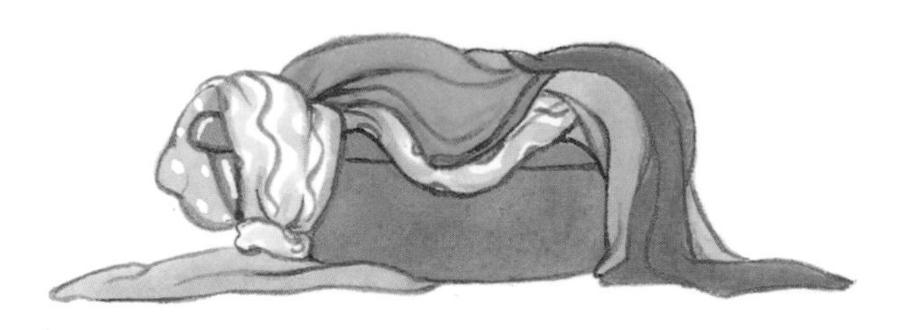

# The Flyaway Laundry

It was a beautiful windy day in Bearborough. Barney really wanted to go and fly his kite up on the hill behind the town, but his mother said that he mustn't go so far on his own, and she was too busy doing the laundry to go with him.

It wasn't like Barney to volunteer to help around the house, but he really wanted to fly his kite, so he made a suggestion. "If I help you with the laundry," he said, "will you come up on the hill with me this afternoon?"

Barney's mother smiled. "That's a good idea," she said, "and look, the first load has just come out of the machine. You can go outside and hang it out for me, while I put the next load in."

The washing basket was very full. It was all the little bear could do to carry it to the line, especially when he got outside and the wind began to push against him. At last, he reached the clothesline and put down the basket.

Oh dear, it wasn't easy! The wild wind tugged at the clothes before Barney could hang them out. And those clothes were really difficult to hold on to. First one of his father's socks went whirling away and over the fence. Then a T-shirt started flapping and flicking Barney on the nose. He held on as hard as he could, but still the T-shirt broke free and sailed away into the flower garden next door.

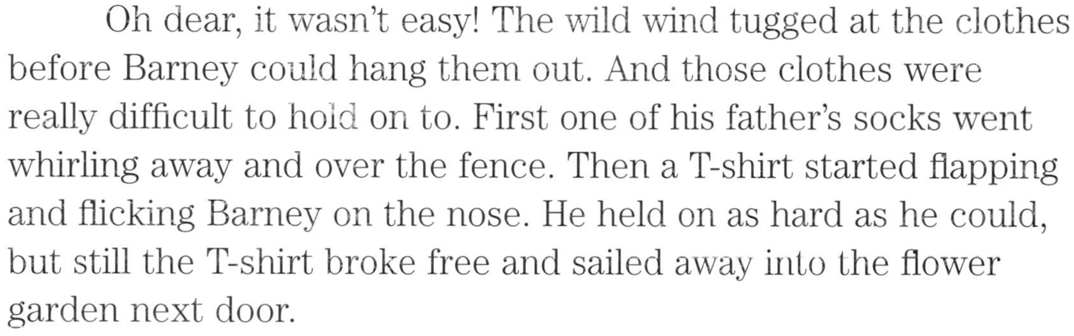

Just then, Barney's mother came out to see how he was doing.

"I'm sorry," gasped Barney, "but I just can't control this laundry!"

He had picked up one of his father's flashier shirts, and it too was struggling to get away.

"Hold on, Barney," cried his mother. "I'll hold on to the other sleeve!"

But as the two bears held on tight to the shirt, determined not to let it escape, the wind puffed into it like a sail and lifted them both off their paws!

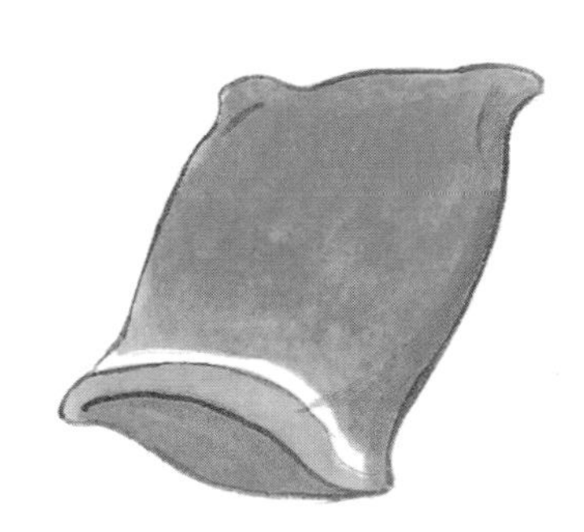

"Don't let go, Barney!" cried his mother, as they sailed into the cabbage field on the other side of the fence.

*"Whee!"* called Barney. "This is better than flying my kite any day!"

The two bears landed with a bump in the field, still holding on to the shirt.

"I think it's too windy for laundry or kite-flying today," laughed Barney's mother, out of breath. "Let's have cocoa and cookies in front of the fire instead!"

# Bears Ahoy!

Ever since their first meeting on the bus home from Bearborough, Barney's granny and Bertram Bear (and his friendly mouse) had been great friends. They liked to take young Barney out and about with them, so the little bear was not surprised when Granny telephoned from Bertram's house to invite Barney on a mystery trip the next day.

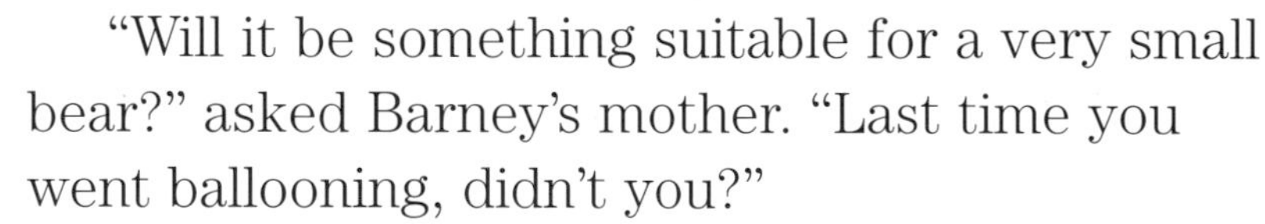

"Will it be something suitable for a very small bear?" asked Barney's mother. "Last time you went ballooning, didn't you?"

Barney couldn't hear what Granny said, but it must have been reassuring, for he heard his mother agreeing that Barney could be called for at half past nine the next morning.

Barney was ready to go when the doorbell rang next day. As soon as he opened the door, he knew that he was in for an exciting day.

"Ahoy there, young bear!" called Granny and Bertram. They were dressed for a day on a boat and seemed determined to talk like old sea bears.

"Don't you worry, me hearty," said Bertram to Mrs. Bear. "We'll bring him back shipshape and no mistake."

Barney was very excited as they walked down the hill. Were they going on a sailing ship? Or a steamer? Or even a fishing boat?

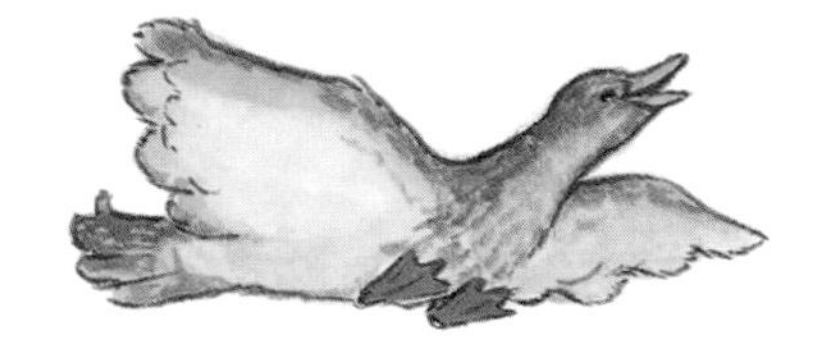

"There she is, the *Ellie May*," said Bertram proudly, as they reached the bridge over the river. "As neat a little craft as you ever did see."

Barney couldn't help feeling a little disappointed when he saw that the *Ellie May* was a very, very small boat!

But Bertram's enthusiasm was catching.

"All aboard," he cried. "We must sail on the next tide!"

"Aye, aye, Captain," called Barney. "Can I be first mate?"

"I'm afraid that job's already taken," said Bertram, winking at Granny, whose ears turned a little pink. "How would you like to be ship's cook?"

Bertram looked uncertain until Granny whispered that this meant being in charge of the sandwiches.

But I'm sorry to report that when they were a long way down the river and the Captain called for lunch, there didn't seem to be many sandwiches left. Barney and Bertram exchanged a long look of understanding.

"Pirates?" asked Bertram.

"Hundreds of 'em, Cap'n!" agreed Barney.

# Are You There?

One wet afternoon, Cleo was very bored. She played with her train set (but some of the track seemed to be missing). She looked at her book about butterflies (but it just made her want to be outside). She bounced on her bed (until her mother stopped her).

"Can't you find something interesting to do?" said her mother, as she watched Cleo straightening her bed.

"No," said Cleo. "There isn't anything."

"Then you can play with your brother," her mother replied. "He's bored too."

Now Cleo loved her baby brother very much, but she had always thought he was much too small to play with. He couldn't do jigsaw puzzles or read books. Although he could crawl about very quickly, he was a little wobbly on his paws, so he wasn't any good at running and jumping games either.

Cleo looked cross. She was just about to say something not very nice about her brother when she saw him, sitting on the floor, peek out at her between his paws.

*"Boo!"* he said.

Cleo smiled. Maybe there was a game she could play with the baby after all. He put his paws over his face once again, and Cleo crept up close and whispered, "Are you there, baby bear?"

With a giggle, the little bear peeked between his paws.

"Es," he said and crawled away.

Cleo thought the game was over, but her little brother pulled his mother's cardigan, which was on a chair, over his head.

"Are you there, baby bear?" called Cleo.

The mound of pink wool swayed from side to side, as if it was shaking its head.

"Oh yes you are!" Cleo whisked the cardigan away, and her brother collapsed into giggles.

Pretty soon, the baby realized that he could hide behind things as well as underneath them. This time, Cleo hid her eyes as he crawled away.

"Are you there, baby bear?" she called.

There was no reply. Cleo had to hunt around the room to find that little bear. As she went, she called, "Where, oh where is baby bear?" and soon found herself making up rhymes to amuse him.

"Where, oh where is baby bear?
Is he here behind the chair?"

It was fun. When the little bears' mother came to call them for supper, neither of them wanted to stop playing, and Cleo has loved her little brother even more from that day to this.

# Mr. Bear the Baker

One morning, Mrs. Bear smiled at Barney and her husband across the breakfast table.

"I'm going shopping with Granny today," she said. "We're both going to buy hats. I want you two boys to take care of the house and of each other."

"We'll be fine," said Mr. Bear. "We've got things we need to do as well," he added mysteriously.

As soon as Mrs. Bear had left the house, Barney's dad hurried him into the kitchen.

"It's your mother's birthday tomorrow," he said, "and I thought we could bake her a cake."

"Us?" asked Barney. "Are we any good at baking?"

"We're the best," said Mr. Bear confidently. "Now we'll both put on these aprons."

Barney felt pretty silly in his apron, but he thought he didn't look as silly as his dad, so it must be fine.

After that, the bears had a wonderful time, weighing and measuring, stirring and mixing.

"I think that's about right," said Mr. Bear, looking suspiciously at the rather odd-looking mixture. "It's time to put it in the oven."

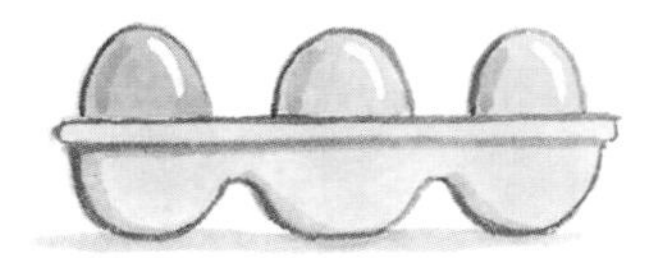

Pretty soon, there was a delicious smell coming from the oven. At least, there was after Mr. Bear remembered to turn it on.

"Time to clean up, Barney," he said. But somehow, both the bears got sidetracked. Mr. Bear felt that he must show his son his egg-juggling routine. And Barney did a lot of useful experiments with flour. In the middle of the mayhem, they heard the front door open.

Barney and his father rushed into the hallway, shutting the kitchen door behind them.

"You can't go in there for a minute," said Mr. Bear firmly to his wife. "We've been doing something extra secret."

Mrs. Bear looked at the two bears in front of her.

"Not much of a secret when most of it is all over your fur," she said, "and if I pay attention to what my nose is telling me, I think it's time something extra secret came out of the oven."

It took Barney and his father the rest of the day to clean up the kitchen—but only ten minutes to help Mrs. Bear eat a very strange-looking but delicious cake the next day!

# The Bravest Bear

One sunny afternoon, Cleo and Barney were playing in Barney's backyard. It was a warm afternoon, so they were pleased when Mrs. Bear brought them glasses of lemonade to drink under the shade of the trees.

As they sat with their cool drinks, Cleo looked up at the branches above.

"Are you afraid of heights, Barney?" she asked.

"Of course not," said Barney. "I can climb ever so high. I'll show you if you like."

And before Cleo could stop him, young Barney was halfway up the tree, sitting on his own special branch.

"Come on up!" he called.

"No, no," said Cleo quickly. "You come down."

"You're not frightened, are you?" asked Barney. "All bears can climb trees. Everyone knows that. Are you a scaredy-bear, Cleo? Scaredy-bear! Scaredy-bear!"

Barney didn't mean to be horrible, but he was so used to finding that Cleo was better at things than he was that he was glad to be able to tease her about something.

Barney made such a fuss about Cleo's climbing that at last she couldn't bear it any longer.

"All right!" she said. "Just watch me!" And she started to climb the tree.

At first it was fine, but as soon as Cleo looked down from the lowest big branch, she began to shiver and shake.

"I don't like it, Barney," she said. "I really am afraid of heights and I want to get down. Will you help me, please?"

"You really are a scaredy-bear!" began Barney. "I'm much braver than you are! Ha ha!"

"I don't think so, Barney," said Mrs. Bear, who had come out to get the empty lemonade glasses. "It took much more courage for Cleo to admit she was afraid than it did for you to climb a tree you have climbed lots of times before."

Barney knew she was right and quickly helped his friend to the ground. Cleo was soon her old self.

"Let's go and hunt for spiders," she said, not noticing that Barney was looking very worried indeed.

# The Park Puzzle

One day, the whole Bear family decided to have a picnic in the park. Mr. and Mrs. Bear were there with Barney, and Granny had brought Bertram along. But after they had enjoyed a picnic of delicious food, all the grown-ups (and Bertram's mouse) fell asleep in the sunshine, and Barney was very bored.

He tried tossing daisies into his father's hat, but had to pretend to be asleep himself when one of them missed and landed on Mr. Bear's nose.

He spent a little time on the swings, but they made him feel a bit sick after such a big lunch.

Finally, Barney wandered off to explore the rest of the park, although he was pretty sure he had been in every part of it already.

But Barney was wrong. Behind some bushes near the tennis courts, he found a little cabin. It was newly painted and had pots of flowers outside. Who could it belong to?

Barney tried the door, but it was locked. He stood on tip-paws and peered into the window, but he couldn't see a thing.

Barney puzzled about the mystery as he walked back to his family. They were all still asleep, except for Bertram, who was decorating Granny's hat with the daisies Barney had picked earlier.

"You look worried," said Bertram, as Barney approached.

"Not worried," said Barney, "just wondering." And he told Bertram all about the little cabin.

"That will be the caretaker's cabin," said Bertram. "The caretaker is an old friend of mine, and I'm pretty sure I know what he'll be doing in there on an afternoon like this. Come with me."

Barney followed Bertram back to the cabin, and Bertram lifted him up to the window. Yes, there was the caretaker, looking as comfortable as can be, and doing just what Barney's family was doing back on the grass.

"I'll never understand grown-up bears," sighed Barney.

# Please, Dad!

When Cleo and her family set off for a weekend away, their little car was packed to the roof with all the things that simply couldn't be left behind. After Cleo's dad's fishing equipment, Cleo's little brother's things and almost all Cleo's toys had been fitted in, Cleo's mother suddenly realized that no one had packed any clothes. Everything had to be taken out and fitted in again, which took all morning.

Even so, there was hardly any room for the bears themselves when it was time to set off. And by then, tempers had become so frayed that Cleo's mother looked grim as she drove down the lane, and her husband looked desperate as he struggled to stop an enormous map from flapping into her face. To be fair, Cleo didn't help at all.

"Please, Dad," she said, when they had been going for ten minutes, "are we there yet?"

"We won't be there until very late at this rate, especially if we go the wrong way," her mother replied between clenched teeth. Her husband was now so entangled with the map that he couldn't speak.

Cleo waited five minutes. "Please, Dad, can we stop?"

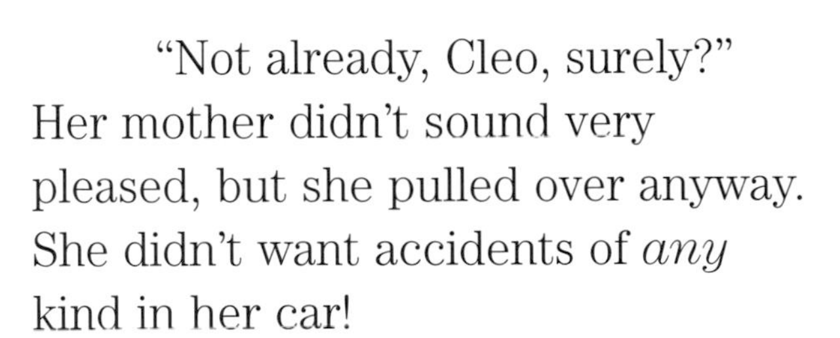

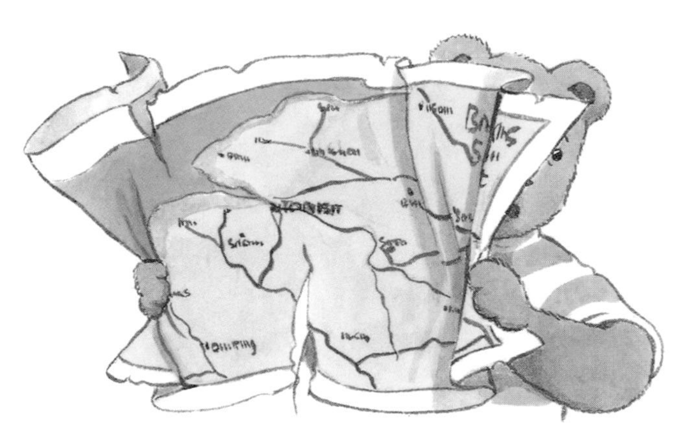

"Not already, Cleo, surely?" Her mother didn't sound very pleased, but she pulled over anyway. She didn't want accidents of *any* kind in her car!

They hadn't been back on the road for more than a minute or two when Cleo piped up again.

"Please, Dad, I think I've forgotten something."

"We haven't forgotten anything," said her mother, "except perhaps how to get there." For Cleo's Dad was flapping the map around in a worrying way.

"Please, Dad," Cleo began.

"If I hear one more word from you," said her mother grimly, "we'll go straight home. Is it right or left here?"

Turning first this way and then that, the family went on for another half hour.

"Please, Dad," said Cleo, "isn't that…?"

Both parents opened their mouths to tell her to be quiet, but the words never came. At the same moment they recognized that they were driving along the familiar lane to their own house. They had been going in a circle.

"Please, Dad," laughed Cleo. "I'm so glad to be home!"

# Bertram's Books

One day, Bertram Bear announced that he was going to have a Grand Clear-out of his house.

"I've got far too much rubbish, collected over the years," he said. "There's hardly room for me in my house, never mind anyone else." And he smiled at Barney's granny.

"Can I help you?" asked Barney. "I'm really good at clearing things out, aren't I, Dad?"

"Last time I let you help me clear out my shed," said his father, "I couldn't find anything for weeks. But if Bertram is willing to take the risk, that's his business."

"Oh, I think we can find something for a small bear to do," said Bertram kindly.

When Barney and Granny arrived at Bertram's house, they soon realized how big the problem was. It looked as though Bertram had never thrown anything away in his life. There were newspapers and boxes everywhere, but most of all there were books on every table and chair and piled up all over the floor.

"I can't resist buying them," said Bertram. "I just love books, you see."

"I quite understand, but why not donate them to the library after you have read them?" suggested Granny. "I'm sure Mr. Leaf would be very grateful."

"How clever you are, my dear, as always," said Bertram.

All afternoon, the bears carried books out to the front of the house, so that the library van could pick them up later.

As Bertram and Granny sat down for a rest, they looked around for Barney. The little bear was nowhere to be seen.

After two hours of frantic searching, Granny was very worried indeed. But just then the van arrived from the library.

"Has anyone lost a small bear?" asked the driver, as he lifted some books from the huge pile.

There was Barney, hidden in a little house of books and enjoying an exciting storybook so much that he hadn't even noticed he had been walled in with books.

"I've heard of bookworms," laughed Bertram, "but it looks as though you and I are both bookbears, young Barney."

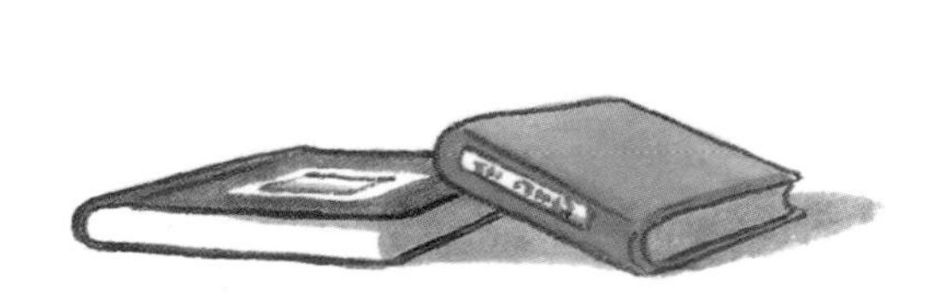

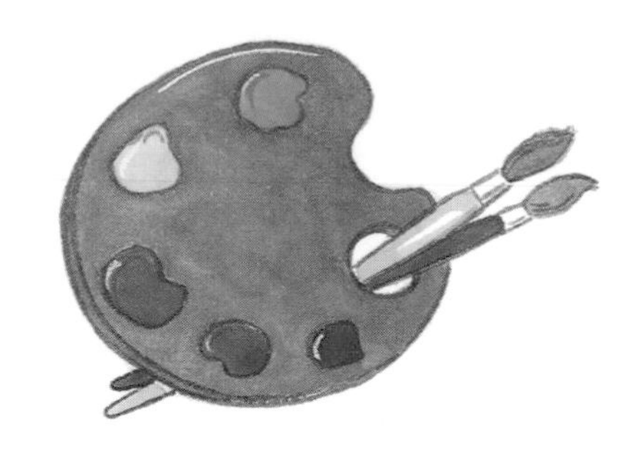

# The Masterpiece

News soon spread around Bearborough that there was to be an Art Show. All bears had to do was send in their pictures. At the end of the show, the best grown-up picture and the best picture by a little bear would receive a prize.

For the next few weeks, there were telltale signs everywhere that most of Bearborough would be entering the competition. Mr. Leaf spent a whole day at the library with a smudge of orange paint on his nose. All the shops in town had run out of paintbrushes, and several bears were seen perched on little stools with sketchbooks.

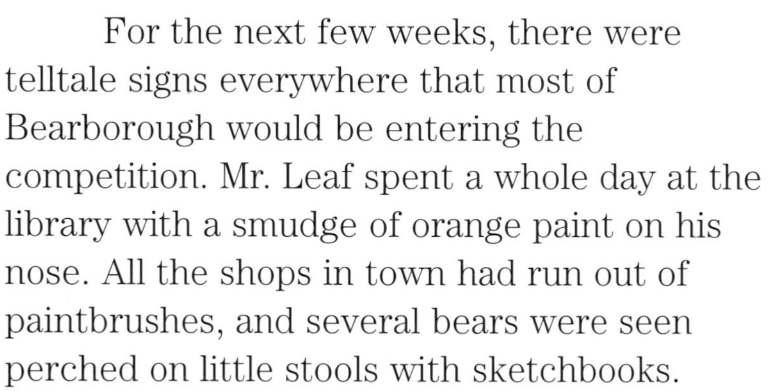

Of course, Barney, Cleo, and their families were all eager to enter the competition. Mr. Bear was particularly anxious to win, but he found it very difficult to find the peace and quiet he needed, he said, for his talent to flourish. When Barney had left pawprints on his fourth sketch (completely by accident, of course), Mr. Bear declared that the shed was the only place he could concentrate properly.

"My work will be very modern," he said, "but I'm sure that is what the judges will be looking for."

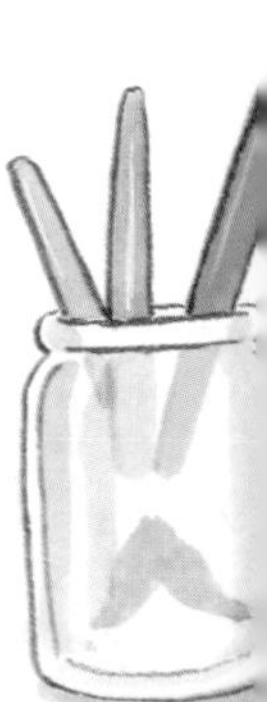

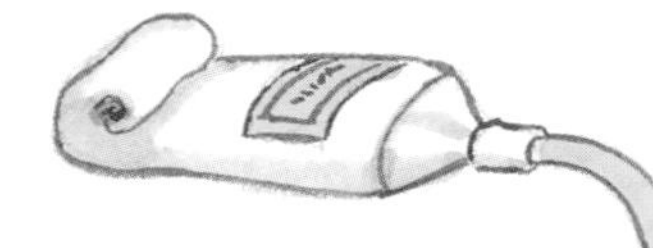

On the day that the pictures had to be submitted, Cleo's mother agreed to take all of them, from both families, in her car. Each picture was framed and wrapped in brown paper, with a label giving the age of the painter. Painters' names were written on the backs of the pictures.

Cleo's mother lay the pictures carefully on the back seat next to Cleo's baby brother's car seat. You can imagine how horrified she was when she arrived to find that the baby bear had spent the whole journey carefully pulling off the labels.

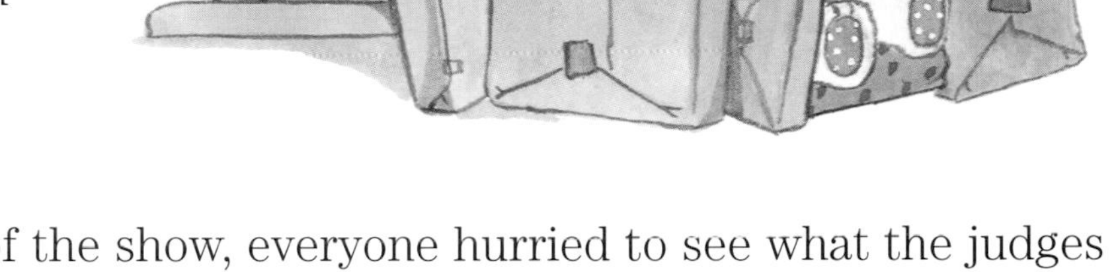

The harassed mother stuck them all back on as well as she could and carried them quickly into the show before anything else could happen to them.

On the last day of the show, everyone hurried to see what the judges had decided. Mrs. Bear went in first with Barney while her husband parked the car.

"Congratulations, sweetheart!" she called when he arrived at last. "You've won first prize!"

Mr. Bear's face lit up with pride, until his wife went on: "in the little bears' competition!"

# Baby Bears

Barney didn't have any brothers and sisters, and he was sorry about that. When he saw Cleo playing with her baby brother, he thought what fun it must be. It made Cleo seem so grown-up and smart. Barney wanted to feel like that too.

"Couldn't we have a baby bear in our family?" he asked his mother one day.

Mr. Bear, who was reading his paper by the fire, overheard Barney's question.

"One little bear is quite enough in this house, rampaging across my vegetable beds and leaving muddy pawprints on the carpet," he laughed, referring to a recent unfortunate incident when Barney had been pretending to be an explorer crossing strange lands.

"Baby bears don't rampage," said Barney. "I was only thinking of a little, tiny baby bear."

"But little bears get bigger," smiled his mother. "Look at the wall where we've measured you from time to time!"

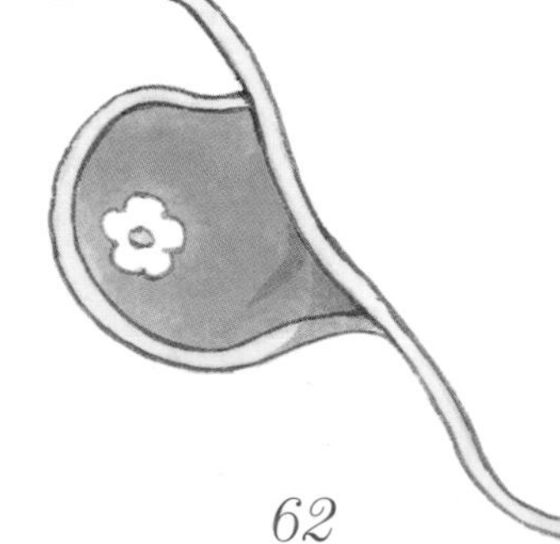

Still, Barney did think it might be better to be part of a bigger family. He decided to go and see Cleo to ask her what she thought.

But when Barney reached Cleo's house, the noise was incredible. Not one, not two, but ten baby bears were crawling and crying and getting up to all sorts of mischief on Cleo's living room carpet, while their parents sat around the table and tried not to notice what was going on.

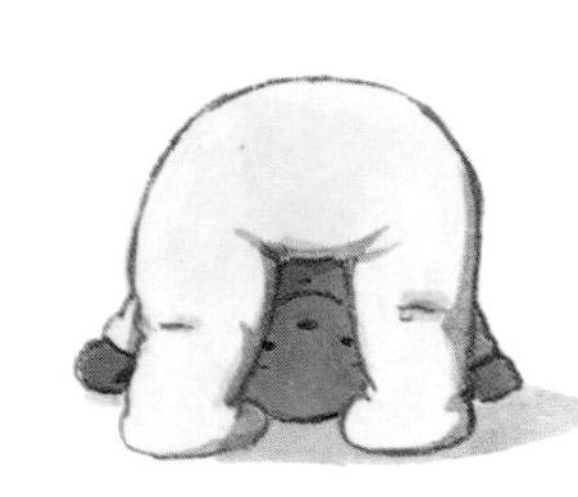

"It's our turn to have the toddlers' group here," Cleo explained above the noise. "It only happens about twice a year, thank goodness!"

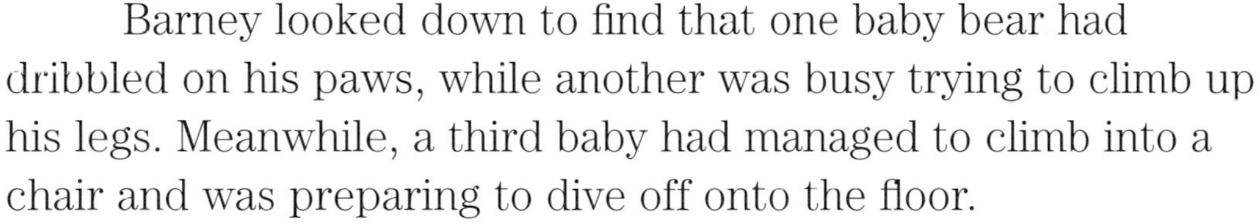

Barney looked down to find that one baby bear had dribbled on his paws, while another was busy trying to climb up his legs. Meanwhile, a third baby had managed to climb into a chair and was preparing to dive off onto the floor.

Barney rushed to save the diving baby, who screamed so loudly when she was picked up that Barney almost dropped her in fright. As he put her gently on the floor, he was just in time to save another baby from eating the leaves of a potted plant.

"Thank you for coming along to help, Barney," said Cleo's mother. "It means that we grown-up bears can have a little rest."

It was Barney who needed a rest when he staggered home an hour later.

"Let's not have any more baby bears," he told his amused parents. "One rampaging little bear in this house is quite enough!"

# A Bunch of Bears

Mr. Bear put down his newspaper. "What did you say, dear?" he asked his wife, who had been giving him a piece of her mind for several minutes.

"I said," repeated Mrs. Bear, "that it is a beautiful day outside. Granny and I have a lot to talk about and plan. We don't need you gentleman bears under our paws all day. Can't you and Bertram take Barney out?"

Bertram, who was comfortably settled in an armchair with an interesting book, looked up at the sound of his name.

Barney, who was happily looking at a nature magazine on the floor, looked up too.

"Let's go," said Mr. Bear with a sigh. "We're not wanted here. Now what can a fine bunch of bears like us find to do on a sunny afternoon?"

The fine bunch of bears wandered off down the road with their hands in their pockets. They watched half a game of tennis in the park. They played half a game of leapbear on the grass. Then they sat down on a bench for a rest.

"I'm exhausted already," said Barney's father. "What I really like to do on a day like this is sit down quietly with my newspaper."

"And what I really like to do is read an exciting book about faraway places," said Bertram Bear.

"And what I really like to do is read my magazine," agreed Barney.

"You know," said Bertram, standing up, "there's somewhere we can do all those things."

Just as Mr. Bear was going to warn Bertram that they really shouldn't go home again yet, Bertram set off firmly in the direction of . . . the library!

The fine bunch of bears spent a lovely afternoon doing what they liked best.

When the three bears returned home that evening, Mrs. Bear and Granny hastily put away the things they were looking at.

"I hope you got lots of exercise and really enjoyed yourselves," said Barney's mother.

"We had a great time," said Mr. Bear. "It's nice to have a change now and then."

# A Perfect Party

Bertram Bear was beside himself with excitement. Now that his house had been improved by Granny's practical paws, and new curtains and carpets had made it look so much more snug and inviting, he felt it was time to give a party. All his friends in Bearborough—and that was a lot of bears!—would be invited.

Granny offered to help with the food and arrangements, but Bertram shook his head firmly. "No, no, my dear. You have done so much hard work on the house. It is my turn to say thank you. Besides, you will be the Most Important Guest, and MIGs can't help as well!"

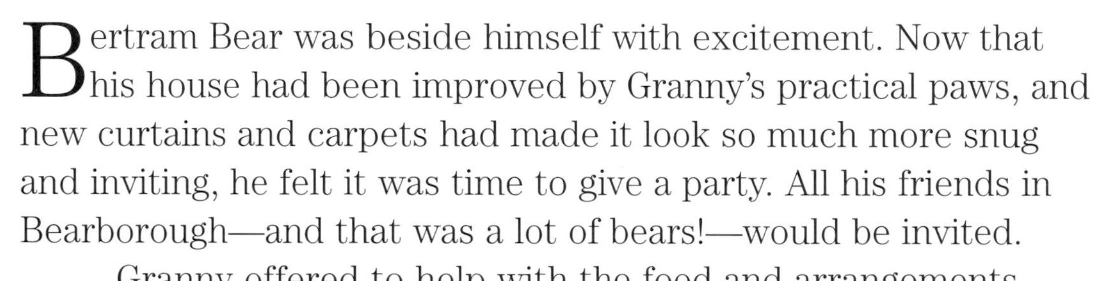

So Bertram got busy. He sent out invitations and made a very efficient list so that he could check who had replied. He spent hours in the kitchen, making all the things that bears love to eat—especially Granny bears. As the day of the party drew near, he even made a big effort with the cleaning and filled his rooms with flowers and balloons. The house looked beautiful.

On the day of the party, when he was sure that everything was perfect, he put on his best suit and sat down to wait for his guests to arrive. He felt a little bit nervous.

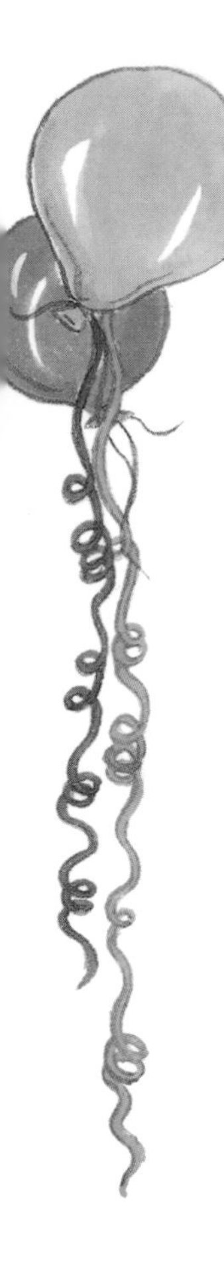

Bertram sat on the stairs. He waited and waited. He could hear the ticking of the clock in the hall. He could feel butterflies fluttering in his tummy. He could see the balloons bobbing in the sunlight that streamed through the window. But he could not hear cars pulling up outside, or guests coming down the path.

The minutes passed . . . and passed . . . and passed. But no one came. Bertram's head drooped, and he fell fast asleep.

*Driiiiing!* Bertram's doorbell woke him. He leaped forward in excitement, but realized as he did so that it was already getting dark—much too late for party guests.

On the doorstep stood Granny. "I know what you said, my dear," she smiled, "but I wondered if you wanted any help for tomorrow."

"Tomorrow?" replied Bertram faintly. Then he opened the door wide and began to laugh.

Next day, every single bear that Bertram had invited hurried over to Bertram's house for his party. This time, Granny did help him to get the food ready—again. She didn't tell a soul, but she shared several secret smiles with Bertram during the evening. And the party? It was perfect!

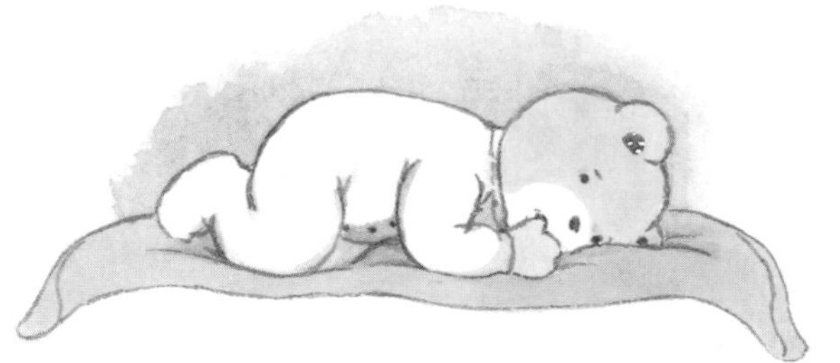

# Poor Bear!

These days, Barney's mother always seemed to be whispering in corners with Granny. It made the little bear feel left out and fed up. One afternoon, he wandered down to Cleo's house, where he felt he was really *appreciated*.

But on this particular afternoon, Cleo told him she was too busy to play. She was wearing her nurse's uniform and looking very important.

"I'm helping to look after my brother," she said. "He's not very well."

"I'm afraid that's true," said Cleo's mother, coming to the door. "Cleo is being my little helper, carrying drinks and snacks up to the baby. Poor bear! It's not serious, but he's not at all well."

Barney looked so forlorn for a moment, that Cleo's mother suggested he should come in anyway for a little while.

"There's some ice cream left over from the invalid," she said. "Maybe you'd like some?"

Barney found that he would like some very much, and as he sat in Cleo's dining room, spooning up ice cream and watching Cleo and her mother preparing nice things for the sick little bear, an idea came to him.

The next morning, bright and early, Barney put his plan into action.

"I'm not feeling well," he told his mother, who was talking to Granny on the phone.

"Ssssh! I can't hear," said Mrs. Bear. "No dear, I think pink would be perfect."

"Pink?" Barney screwed up his nose.

"I'm not talking to you, Barney," said his mother. "I'm talking to Granny."

"But I'm not well," moaned Barney, clutching his tummy.

Mrs. Bear put down the phone and put one paw on Barney's forehead.

"It's nothing serious," she said. "Eat up."

"But it *hurts*!" groaned her little bear, holding his head.

"It was your tummy a minute ago," said his mother grimly. "Where does it hurt exactly?"

"All over," mumbled Barney, "all the time."

"This isn't like you, Barney." Mrs. Bear looked thoughtful. "Poor bear! I wonder if it might be because I haven't had much time recently to talk to my best little bear? How would it be if I told you a Very Big Secret?" And, as Barney went to hug her knees, Mrs. Bear leaned down and whispered in his furry ear.

Barney's eyes were wide with surprise. "Does Granny know?" he asked.

"Yes, of course," laughed his mother. "Now, are you still feeling ill?"

"Who, me?" said naughty Barney. "Never!"

# Martha Makes a Wish

One morning, Barney carried a cup of coffee and a bowl of cereal along to his granny's room, so that she could have breakfast in bed. He did spill quite a bit on the way, but he hoped it would disappear into the carpet before his mother saw it.

"I thought I should have a practice," Barney told Granny, "before next week."

"Why?" teased Granny. "What's happening next week?"

"But I thought you knew!" cried Barney, his eyes open wide. "You're going to marry Bertram!"

"So I am," laughed Granny. "So you're going to bring me breakfast in bed on my wedding day, are you?"

"Yes," said Barney, "and every day after that."

"But Barney," said Granny gently, "hasn't anyone told you? After that, I'll be living at Bertram's house."

Barney's face fell. He hadn't thought about that at all. He really liked having Granny living at home.

"I wish you could stay here," he said. "I wish you weren't getting married at all!" And he buried his face in the bedclothes and burst into tears.

Granny cuddled the little bear. "I'm going to tell you a story," she said, "about a bear called Martha. When she was quite young, she met a wonderful gentleman bear called Edward. He asked her to marry him, and she said yes. They didn't have much money, but they were very happy. They had a little girl bear and a little boy bear, and they helped them to grow up into fine young bears. Then, just as they were looking forward to a peaceful time together, Edward died and left Martha all alone. She was so very sad, she thought she would never be happy again, although she had a lovely family and a dear little grandson. She wished for the sun to shine for her again. And one day, Martha was very lucky indeed. She met a funny bear with a mouse in his hat. His wife had died, too. Pretty soon, Martha couldn't imagine life without the funny bear. Bertram felt the same, so he and Martha thought they would get married. They both felt they were the luckiest bears in the world to have a second chance to be happy. Now do you understand, honey?"

"Yes," whispered Barney. "But I didn't know your name was Martha."

"Well, now you do," smiled Granny. "Mmmmm! What a *delicious* breakfast!"

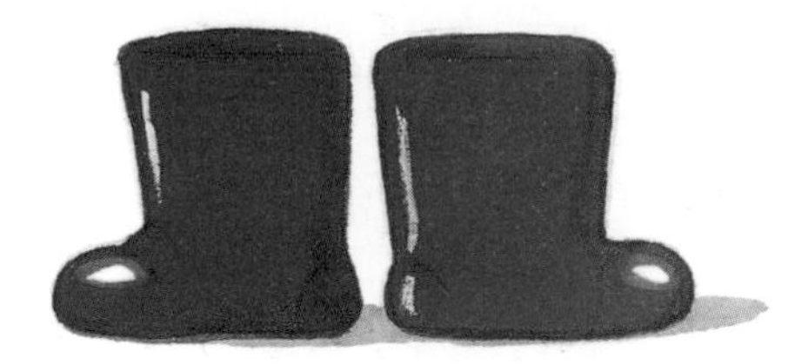

# Granny Bear's Boots

There are a lot of things to be organized before a wedding, but Granny and Barney's mother between them managed to sort everything out. Then, one evening at supper, Granny suddenly put down her mug with a crash.

"What if it rains?" she cried.

"We can have everything inside," said Mrs. Bear calmly. "There's no problem at all."

"Oh yes there is," declared Granny Bear. "I still have to get out of the car. What if there are puddles for my beautiful new shoes? What if it rains on my wonderful wedding hat?"

For the first time during all the preparations, Mr. Bear said something useful.

"My dear," he smiled, "I will personally go into town and buy you the loveliest umbrella I can find. You'll hope it *does* rain when you see it. But I really don't know what to do about your shoes. A little bit of water won't hurt them, will it?"

"It will *ruin* them," said Granny firmly.

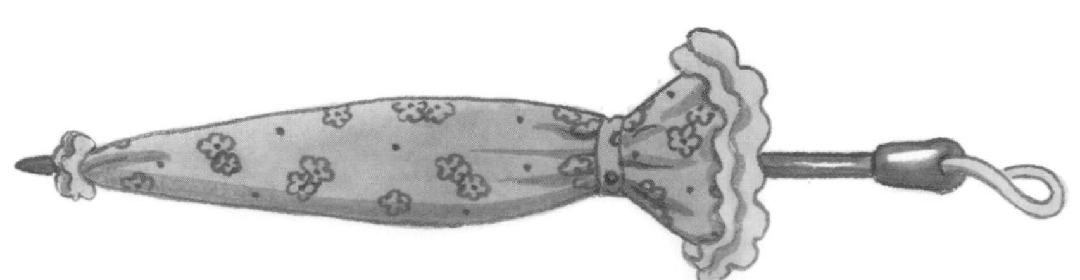

Of course, Barney had been listening to this conversation, and he hurried off to tell Cleo about the problem.

"What she needs is a good pair of boots," said Cleo, "but I don't think you can get special waterproof wedding boots."

The two little bears sat in silence for a moment.

"I know!" cried Cleo. "We can decorate her ordinary boots. It will be fun. Come on!"

Cleo found paints, paper, sequins, and even some ribbons, while Barney crept off to "borrow" the boots. Then he and Cleo had a lovely time decorating the boots with everything they could find.

"It can be a surprise," said Barney. "I'll just put them back and wait for Granny to notice."

But Granny noticed sooner than he had guessed. That evening, Bertram came by to take Granny for a walk by the river. The ground was a little damp, so Granny hurried off to put on her boots—and came back wearing them and roaring with laughter.

Bertram was puzzled, until Granny explained about the wedding and the rain.

"It was a lovely idea, Barney," she said. "But what will people think if I wear them now?"

"Sweetheart, they will think you look beautiful," said Bertram. "And as for the wedding, you don't have to worry. Naturally, the groom will carry the bride—like this!" And to Barney's amazement, the sprightly old bear scooped up Granny and carried her off—boots and all!

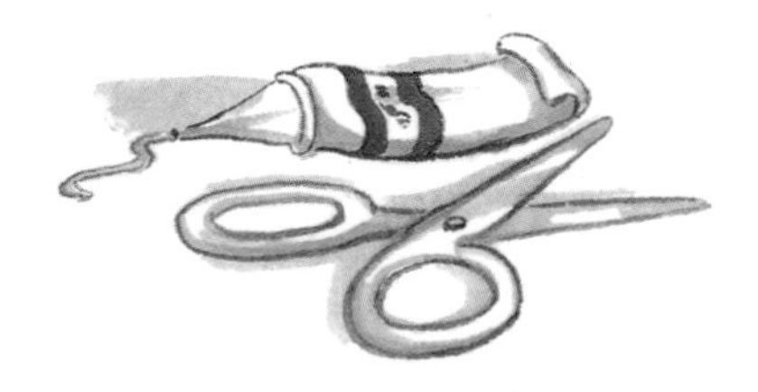

# The Bouncing Bear

Cleo and Barney were training for their school sports day. Well, "training" was the name they gave to running about in the park (as they usually did) and jumping on and off of the benches (as they usually did) and seeing who could swing the highest (as they usually did).

"I love swinging," said Cleo as she flew to and fro one day. "You can see all sorts of things that you can't see when you're standing on the ground."

"Yes," said Barney, as he swung past, "like trees and bushes and bouncing bears. Yes, look, a bouncing bear!"

It was true. Every few seconds, the smiling face of a bear appeared above the bushes opposite. Then he dropped down out of sight again. The next time he appeared, he waved!

Cleo waved back, but Barney was not looking so happy. He let his swing go slower and slower until he put his paws on the ground and stopped.

"I recognize that bear," he said. "It's Bingo from school. He's younger than us, Cleo, but look how high he's jumping! I thought I was the best jumper!"

"You are, Barney," said Cleo loyally, but as she watched the bear appear above the bushes over and over again, she had to admit that even Barney couldn't possibly jump so high.

"We should say hello anyway," said Cleo firmly. "Come on."

But as they walked around the bushes, Cleo and Barney started laughing. Bingo wasn't jumping by himself. He had a trampoline!

"Come and try it!" shouted the little bear. "Dad gave it to me for my birthday. I love it!"

Soon three little bears were bouncing higher than they had ever bounced before—and turning somersaults and doing backflips. They had a wonderful time.

Just recently, Mrs. Bear wondered why her bed springs seem to have lost their spring. I think I can guess. Can you?

# Ready, Set, Go!

School sports day arrived at last, and Barney was determined to do his best. The whole family was coming to watch him. Barney hoped that his father wouldn't call out or do anything embarrassing, and he made his mother promise not to wear a hat. Granny, he knew, always wore hats to go out, but then she was a fairly old bear, so maybe his friends wouldn't think that was odd.

All too soon, Mr. Tedson was blowing his whistle for the first race. "All bears to the starting line! Ready, set, go!"

Barney ran as fast as he could, but just as he reached the finish line, Cleo came sailing past him and won the race.

"Well done, Cleo," puffed Barney. He didn't like to be beaten, but if it had to be anyone, then he would rather his best friend was the winner than any other little bear.

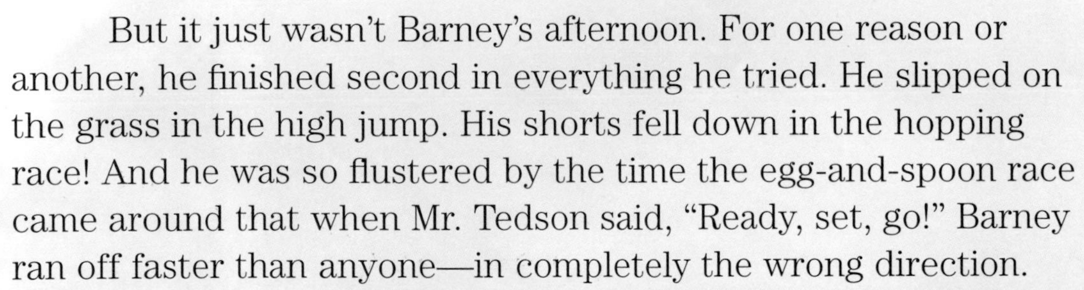

But it just wasn't Barney's afternoon. For one reason or another, he finished second in everything he tried. He slipped on the grass in the high jump. His shorts fell down in the hopping race! And he was so flustered by the time the egg-and-spoon race came around that when Mr. Tedson said, "Ready, set, go!" Barney ran off faster than anyone—in completely the wrong direction.

By the time the last race was called, Barney had given up. He knew that he wouldn't win anything all day long. And to make matters worse, as all the little bears got ready on the starting line, a large butterfly came and landed on Barney's nose. Barney didn't want to hurt it, so he concentrated very hard and blew ever so gently. The butterfly fluttered safely away, just as Mr. Tedson was saying, "…set, go!"

Maybe it was because concentrating on the butterfly had calmed Barney's nerves, or maybe it was because he had stopped trying quite so hard, but Barney ran the race of his life. He sailed over the finish line in front of all the other bears.

"Barney! Barney! Barney!" came a loud chant from the crowd, but Barney was so happy to have won that even his dad couldn't embarrass him as he held his winning cup as high as his paws could reach.

# The Very Best Bear

Granny Bear need not have worried. When Barney brought her breakfast in bed (and managed not to spill a single drop) on her wedding morning, the sun was shining and there wasn't a cloud in the sky.

Much to Mrs. Bear's amazement, everything was right on schedule. Granny's flowers arrived on time, and Barney managed to get dressed *and* put on his bow tie without any mishaps. Even Mr. Bear was ready as the special car drew up at the front door.

But just as the Bear family was leaving the house, the telephone rang. Granny looked concerned, as Barney's mother hurried to answer it.

"Don't worry, we'll think of something," the others heard her say, as she put the phone down.

In the car, Mrs. Bear explained that Bertram's best bear's car had broken down, and he wouldn't be able to make it in time for the wedding.

"What's a best bear?" asked Barney.

"It's a special friend of the bridegroom," explained his father. "My best bear was Uncle George."

"Maybe you could be the best bear, Dad," said Barney.

"Well, that's really for Bertram to decide," replied his father. "But anyway, I've already got a job. I'm giving Granny away."

Barney thought that was pretty funny, until his parents explained that it was just a way of showing that Granny was going to be part of a new family with Bertram.

Bertram was waiting on the steps, as the Bear family arrived. And he didn't look worried at all.

"You seem to have solved your problem," said Mr. Bear.

"I have now," said Bertram. "I've decided to ask the bear who brought Martha and me together to be our best bear. And I couldn't think of a better bear to do it, so he really *is* the best. Come on, Barney, it's time to go!"

So Granny's happiest day was Barney's proudest day, too, and most of their friends from Bearborough were there to make sure that it certainly was a day to remember.

# Index of Themes